101 DALMATIANS

Illustrated by the Disney Storybook Artists
Based on the book *The Hundred and One Dalmatians* by Dodie Smith,
published by The Viking Press
Adapted by Kate Hannigan

© Disney Enterprises, Inc.
Visit our Web site at www.disneybooks.com

Published by
Louis Weber, C.E.O.
Publications International, Ltd.
7373 North Cicero Avenue
Lincolnwood, Illinois 60712

www.pilbooks.com

Manufactured in China.

8 7 6 5 4 3 2 1

ISBN: 0-7853-9544-X

In a cozy house in London there lived two happy
couples. Roger and Anita liked music and long walks.
Pongo and Perdita liked long walks, too. They also liked to
wag their tails and eat special treats from Nanny.

One day, Pongo and Perdita were waiting patiently for their humans to take them on a walk in the park. Suddenly, a red car came roaring up to the house. Before they could bark, the front door burst open. There stood Cruella De Vil!

Cruella was Anita's old friend from school, but that didn't matter to Perdita. Perdita didn't like Cruella and ran to the kitchen to hide.

Cruella walked all around the house in her fluffy fur coat and pointy shoes. "I live for furs!" she shouted. "I worship furs!" She was looking for Pongo and Perdita's puppies.

Anita told her that the puppies hadn't been born yet. Cruella was disappointed and made Anita promise to tell her when the puppies arrived.

After Cruella left, Pongo went to find Perdita where she was hiding. "That devil woman wants our puppies," Perdita cried.

Pongo told her everything would be all right. He said Roger and Anita knew Cruella was up to something. But that didn't help Perdita. She was afraid of Cruella.

On a stormy night a few weeks later, the puppies were born! Pongo and Roger waited anxiously in the kitchen for some news. Finally Nanny raced into the room.

"Eight puppies!" she called, hurrying back to Perdita and Anita. Pongo and Roger jumped for joy! "Make that thirteen! Fourteen!" she shouted again. "Oh my, fifteen!"

Pongo was dizzy with excitement. He was the father of fifteen puppies! Anita and Nanny brought one of them out to show Pongo. Together they all danced with delight.

Suddenly thunder crashed, and lightning lit up the night sky. The back door flew open, and a figure stood in the doorway. It was Cruella De Vil!

"Fifteen puppies!" laughed Cruella. She was excited too, but not for Pongo and Perdita. She had other plans for those puppies.

Cruella peeked inside the blanket of one of the newborns. The puppy was completely white — there were no spots. Cruella shouted in disappointment. She wanted puppies with lots of spots!

Nanny explained to Cruella that the puppies would get their spots soon enough. They had to get just a bit older. Cruella was glad to hear that. She reached into her purse and pulled out her wallet. Cruella wanted to buy all of the puppies! "How much for the puppies?" she asked.

Anita told her they couldn't give them up. "Poor Perdita, she'd be heartbroken," she said. But Cruella insisted. She started to write a check, shaking her pen and splattering ink onto Roger and Pongo.

"When can the puppies leave their mother?" she asked.

"Never," said Roger. He told Cruella they weren't selling the puppies—not a single one.

Cruella De Vil was furious. She stormed out of the house in a rage!

The puppies were happy together. They loved to play and watch their favorite TV shows with their parents. They especially liked to bark at the bad guys. At bedtime, Pongo and Perdita took walks with Roger and Anita. Nanny tucked the puppies into bed each night.

One evening as the two couples strolled to the park, they passed an old truck in the shadows. Inside the truck sat two men who worked for Cruella — Horace and Jasper. They were waiting until Pongo and Perdita and their humans rounded the corner. Then they pushed their way into the house.

Nanny tried to chase them out, but it was too late! Horace and Jasper took off with the puppies!

The next morning, Cruella read about the dognapping in the newspaper. She laughed and laughed. She picked up the phone and called Anita, pretending to be sad for her.

Roger had a bad feeling about Cruella. He and Anita didn't know what to do next.

Pongo and Perdita knew their humans tried everything to find the puppies. "Now it's up to us dogs," he said. He told Perdita about the Twilight Bark. He would bark his message about the stolen puppies to the dogs of London. They would hear it and pass it on.

As they walked that evening with Roger and Anita, the dogs stopped at the top of a hill. Pongo began to bark as loud as he could. He hoped the Twilight Bark would carry his message to someone who could help.

The news passed quickly. Eventually it reached a quiet farm in the countryside, far from London. An old horse and stray cat heard the message first.

The cat, called Sergeant Tibs, ran to wake up the Old English sheepdog. "Colonel, there's a vital message coming in from London!" Tibs said.

The Colonel listened to the alert. "Fifteen spotted puddles stolen!" he said. Tibs said maybe it was puppies, not puddles. The Colonel agreed. "That's terrible!" he said.

Sergeant Tibs recalled hearing barking at the old De Vil place nearby. The Colonel said they should investigate. They marched right over to the spooky old house.

As Tibs peered through the dusty windows, he noticed a hole in a wall. He climbed through it, and that's when he saw them. Not just the fifteen missing puppies, but many more! There were spotted puppies everywhere!

Tibs began to count. And count and count. Ninety-nine puppies! He couldn't believe it! Suddenly, Horace and Jasper grabbed for him. He had to get out of there fast.

Sergeant Tibs raced back to the Colonel, and they spread the word about the puppies. The Twilight Bark carried the news all the way back to Pongo and Perdita. The puppies were found!

When Pongo and Perdita heard the message, they left
home right away. There was no time to lose. They ran
through fields of snow and swam through rivers of ice.
Nothing could keep them from their puppies!

Inside the old De Vil mansion, Cruella was shouting at Horace and Jasper. She wanted to make fur coats out of the puppies! "I'll be back first thing in the morning!" she told them. "You better get some work done."

Horace and Jasper didn't want to do Cruella's work. They just wanted to watch their favorite TV show. After Cruella left, they sat back down in front of the television.

That's when Sergeant Tibs sneaked into the room. He had to act fast and quietly. Whispering to the puppies, he told them to climb through the hole in the wall and escape. Horace and Jasper kept watching TV. They didn't notice a thing as ninety-nine puppies tiptoed past.

Just as the puppies started to squeeze through the hole, Horace and Jasper leapt to their feet. They chased the puppies all around the house, up the stairs and down again!

Suddenly Pongo and Perdita crashed through the windows. They fought Horace and Jasper as Sergeant Tibs and the Colonel led the puppies to safety.

Pongo and Perdita were so happy to see their puppies again. But they knew they weren't out of danger. Cruella and her workers were still after them!

Pongo led the puppies onto a frozen river. They walked on the ice so they wouldn't leave tracks for Horace and Jasper to follow. Before long, they met a black Labrador who could help them escape. The Labrador had arranged a ride back to London for Pongo, Perdita, and all of their ninety-nine puppies.

The Labrador showed Pongo and Perdita a van that was waiting nearby. As they talked, some of the puppies fell into ashes from a blacksmith's fireplace. They were getting so dirty!

Pongo looked at the messy puppies. He was about to scold them when he got a wonderful idea. "Hurry, children, get as dirty as you can!" he said.

Pongo, Perdita, and the puppies rolled in the black soot. They were covered from head to tail. They didn't look like Dalmatians anymore — they looked like Labradors! Cruella would never catch them now, Pongo hoped.

With the puppies in their dark disguises, it was time to sneak into the van. They walked right under the noses of Horace and Jasper. Soon Cruella drove by in her bright red car. She stared at the black puppies. "It couldn't be," she said to herself.

As the last group of dogs walked toward the van, the snow began to melt. It dripped onto the puppies' backs, washing away the soot. Cruella saw the Dalmatians' spots. "They're escaping!" she shouted.

The van took off, and Pongo and Perdita jumped aboard at the last moment. They were on their way back home! But Cruella and her workers were right behind them.

Cruella raced behind the van in her bright red car. Horace and Jasper followed in their old truck. It was a wild chase. Cruella even plowed into a pile of snow.

Finally she crashed right into Horace and Jasper's truck. Cruella waved her fists in the air and shouted as the puppies got away!

The puppies made it home safely to London. Nanny happily counted them. They were all there—plus a whole lot more!

Roger and Anita couldn't believe it. Ninety-nine puppies, plus Pongo and Perdita. That made 101 Dalmatians! What in the world were they going to do with so many puppies?

"We'll have a plantation," Roger said. "A Dalmatian plantation!" Roger sat at the piano and began to sing. Anita joined in, along with Pongo, Perdita, and all the puppies. They had a howling good time!